6 7
16 17 19 20
26 27 28 29 30
36 37 38 39 40
46 47 48 49 50
56 57 58 59 60
66 67 68 69 70
76 77 78 79 80
86 87 88 89 90
96 97 98 99 100
KT-385-385

For the children and teachers of Larkrise Primary School, Oxford. T.H.

For Beth, Becky and Caz. S.H.

First published 2018 by Walker Books Ltd, 87 Vauxhall Walk, London SE11 5HJ

2 4 6 8 10 9 7 5 3 1

Text © 2018 Teresa Heapy   Illustrations © 2018 Sue Heap

The right of Teresa Heapy and Sue Heap to be identified as author and illustrator respectively of this work has been asserted by them in accordance with the Copyright, Designs and Patents Act 1988

This book has been typeset in Youbee

Printed in China

All rights reserved. No part of this book may be reproduced, transmitted or stored in an information retrieval system in any form or by any means, graphic, electronic or mechanical, including photocopying, taping and recording, without prior written permission from the publisher.

British Library Cataloguing in Publication Data:
a catalogue record for this book is available from the British Library

ISBN 978-1-4063-7789-7 (hardback)
ISBN 978-1-4063-8564-9 (paperback)

www.walker.co.uk

Ten Cars and a Million Stars

A Counting Storybook

Teresa Heapy
illustrated by Sue Heap

WALKER BOOKS
AND SUBSIDIARIES
LONDON • BOSTON • SYDNEY • AUCKLAND

Alice was doing her
best counting for the baby.

"Look, Baby,"
she said.

"Here is **ONE** giant teddy."

"You've got **TWO** floppy bunnies

and **THREE**
shaky rattles ...

and *I've* got **FOUR** smart

penguins, **FIVE** cuddly cats,

SIX friendly monkeys,

SEVEN shy ducks,

EIGHT tiny mice
and NINE big dinosaurs.

Here are **TEN** fast cars, stuck

in a long traffic jam ...

and **TWENTY** silly animals

with **THIRTY** hats

and **FORTY** shoes!

There are **FIFTY** blocks

in our secret den, and ...

this many toys make

ONE HUNDRED!"

The baby was very impressed.

7
1
6
5
9
10
8

But Alice wasn't finished. "There are bigger numbers than that, Baby. There are thousands of snowflakes in a snowstorm. And millions of stars in the sky!"

Just then Mummy came in.
"We've been doing counting, Mummy," said Alice.

"Mummy! Hug!" said the baby.

“Can I have a hug, too?”
asked Alice.

Mummy opened her arms
and she smiled a big smile.
"Not just one," she said.
"More hugs than you can
EVER count!"

1	2	3	4	5
11	12	13	14	15
21	22	23	24	25
31	32	33	34	35
41	42	43	44	45
51	52	53	54	55
61	62	63	64	65
71	72	73	74	75
81	82	83	84	85
91	92	93	94	95